RAINBOW magic ®

The Party Fairies

D0012581

To Ellie Delamere who loves fairies

Special thanks to
Narinder Dhami

ORCHARD BOOKS
338 Euston Road, London NW1 3BH
Orchard Books Australia
Hachette Children's Books
Level 17/207 Kent Street, Sydney, NSW 2000
A Paperback Original
First published in Great Britain in 2005
Text © Working Partners Limited 2005
Created by Working Partners Limited, London W6 0QT
Illustrations © Georgie Ripper 2004
The right of Georgie Ripper to be identified as the illustrator
of this work has been asserted by her in accordance
with the Copyright, Designs and Patents Act, 1988.
A CIP catalogue record for this book is available
from the British Library.
ISBN 1 84362 820 1
11
Printed in Great Britain

Grace
the Glitter
Fairy

by Daisy Meadows

illustrated by Georgie Ripper

ORCHARD BOOKS

www.rainbowmagic.co.uk

A Very Special Party Invitation

Our gracious King and gentle Queen
Are loved by fairies all.
One thousand years have they ruled well,
Through troubles great and small.

In honour of their glorious reign
A party has been planned,
To celebrate their jubilee
Throughout all Fairyland.

The party is a royal surprise,
We hope they'll be delighted.
So shine your wand and press your dress...
For you have been invited!

RSVP: HRH THE FAIRY GODMOTHER

Contents

A Party Afoot

"Isn't it a beautiful day?" Kirsty Tate said happily, looking up at the deep blue sky. "I'm so glad you're staying here for a whole week, Rachel."

Kirsty was sitting on the grass in the Tates' back garden, making a daisy chain with her best friend, Rachel Walker. Pearl, Kirsty's black and white kitten, was snoozing in a patch of sunshine in the middle of the path.

"You know, Rachel," Kirsty went on, picking another daisy. "This is the perfect day for—"

"A party!" Rachel broke in, knowing exactly what Kirsty was going to say.

Kirsty nodded, a frown on her face. "Let's hope horrid Jack Frost's goblins don't spoil someone's special day."

"The Party Fairies will do their best to stop them," Rachel replied in a determined voice. "And so will we."

Rachel and Kirsty had a wonderful secret which no one else in the whole human world knew about. They were best friends with the fairies! So far, the girls had helped the Rainbow Fairies and the Weather Fairies against Jack Frost's evil spells. Now it was the turn of the Party Fairies.

"Isn't it just like mean old Jack Frost to want to spoil everyone's fun?" said Kirsty. "He can't stop causing trouble, even though he's been banished to his ice castle."

"If he hadn't been such a pest, he could have come to the surprise party for the Fairy King and Queen's 1000th jubilee," Rachel pointed out.

The girls had been invited to the
Fairyland party themselves, and they
had been very excited about it – until
they found out that Jack Frost was
determined to have a party of his own.
His goblins were causing trouble at
human parties, so that the Party Fairies
would appear to put things right. Then
the goblins would try to steal the fairies'
magic party bags for Jack Frost to use
at his party.

"Well, we managed to keep Cherry
the Cake Fairy and Melodie
the Music Fairy's party
bags safe," Kirsty said,
adding another daisy
to her chain. "We'll
just have to keep
our eyes open."

"And our ears," added Rachel.

Suddenly, there was a scrabbling
noise behind the hedge. "OW!"
someone muttered.
"That hurt."

"Who was
that?" gasped
Rachel.
"Do you
think it was
a goblin?"

Kirsty grinned
and shook her head.
"It's OK," she said. "It sounds like
Mr Cooper, our next-door neighbour."

At that moment, Mr Cooper popped
his head over the hedge. He was a tall,
thin man with a cheerful smile. "Sorry,
Kirsty," he said, "did I startle you?

I pricked my finger on the rosebush."
He held up a small parcel wrapped in
shiny blue paper. "I'm trying to hide
these presents around the garden for the
treasure hunt this afternoon."

"Treasure hunt?" repeated Rachel,
looking puzzled.

Mr Cooper nodded. "Yes, it's my son
Jamie's birthday today," he replied.
"He's five and we're having a party."

A party! Rachel and
Kirsty glanced
at each other
in excitement.

"We've got ten
children coming,"
Mr Cooper went on.
"And we've hired a clown called
Mr Chuckles. Jamie is really excited."
He smiled and shook his head.
"It's going to be a lot of hard
work, though."

Rachel nudged Kirsty, who knew
exactly what her friend was thinking.

"Maybe Rachel and I could come
over and give you and Mrs Cooper
a hand?" Kirsty suggested.

"Yes, we'd love to," Rachel
added eagerly.

Mr Cooper's face lit up. "That's very kind of you," he beamed. "Jamie would love that. The guests are arriving at three o'clock, so could you come at two?"

"Of course we will," Rachel and Kirsty said together.

Mr Cooper gave them a grateful smile, and went off to hide some more parcels.

Kirsty turned to Rachel, her eyes wide with excitement. "Do you think a goblin will turn up and try to spoil Jamie's party?" she asked.

"I don't know," Rachel replied. "But if one does, we'll be ready for him!"

Decorating Difficulties

"This is going to be fun," Kirsty grinned, as she rang the Coopers' doorbell. "Jamie is really sweet. It'll be a bit noisy, though, with him and all his friends running around enjoying themselves."

"Maybe they'll frighten the goblins away!" Rachel said with a laugh.

The front door opened. A small boy with exactly the same cheerful smile as Mr Cooper stood in the hallway.

"Hello, Kirsty," Jamie called eagerly. "Are you and your friend here to help with my party?"

"Yes, we are," Kirsty replied, smiling and handing Jamie a parcel. "Happy birthday."

Jamie tore off the wrapping paper excitedly and beamed when he saw the bright red car inside. "Thank you! Come on," he said, taking Kirsty's hand. "Me and Mummy are putting up decorations in the lounge."

Rachel and Kirsty followed him down the hallway. Mrs Cooper was standing on a chair, pinning a HAPPY BIRTHDAY banner to the wall.

"Hello, Kirsty," she smiled. "And it's Rachel, isn't it? It's so kind of you to help out. Thank you."

"Mum!" Jamie was dancing around the lounge, waving his new car. "Look what Kirsty and Rachel gave me! And can we put up the streamers now? Can we?"

"There's still an hour to go and he's already fizzing with excitement," Mrs Cooper said, laughing. "Would you girls be able to put up the streamers and balloons, please, while I go and help Jamie's dad finish off the food?" She pointed to a folded, gold-coloured paper tablecloth, and some bowls and plates which were on the table. "And if you have time, could you lay the table, too?"

"Of course we can," Rachel replied.

Mrs Cooper thanked the girls and hurried off to the kitchen.

Jamie grabbed the box of decorations from the sofa. "Daddy bought some new extra-long streamers," said Jamie proudly. "They're gold and silver – look!"

He began unrolling one of the streamers. But before he had got very far, a piece about fifty centimetres long dropped off and floated to the ground.

"Oh!" Jamie gasped.

"I'm sure the rest of it is OK," Rachel said quickly.

"Keep going, Jamie."

But as Jamie unrolled the streamer, more lengths of brightly-coloured paper fell off. Rachel opened the other packets, but those streamers had been spoiled in exactly the same way.

"It's just as if someone has cut the streamers and then rolled them back up again," Kirsty whispered to Rachel.

Rachel nodded solemnly. "Do you think it could be goblin mischief?" she asked.

Jamie was looking close to tears.

"They're too short!" he wailed.

"Don't worry, Jamie,"
Kirsty said, giving him
a hug. "I've got just
the thing to fix this.
I won't be long."

Kirsty ran home
and found a big
roll of sparkly, blue
sticky-tape, which was
left over from Christmas. Then
she went back to the Coopers' house
and showed it to Jamie. "Look,"
she said, beginning to stick the pieces
of one of the streamers together.
"Now you'll have stripy gold, silver
and blue streamers."

Jamie's face lit up. "They look even
better now!" he declared happily.

The three of them quickly stuck the rest of the streamers together and then Rachel and Kirsty began to pin them up around the room. They had just finished when there was a ring at the doorbell.

"That'll be Mr Chuckles," Mrs Cooper called from the kitchen. "Could you let him in, please, Kirsty?"

"I think Jamie has beaten me to it," Kirsty chuckled, as Jamie dashed past her into the hall.

Rachel and Kirsty followed him, and found the clown standing on the doorstep, smiling down at Jamie. He wore a bright blue, baggy suit and a blue bowler hat.

"You must be the birthday boy," he said.

"Where's your big red nose and your big clown shoes, Mr Chuckles?" Jamie wanted to know. Rachel and Kirsty smiled.

"Ah, well, I'm not quite ready yet," Mr Chuckles explained. "It's difficult to drive my van in big clown shoes."

Looking as if he was about to burst with excitement, Jamie ran to tell his mum about the clown.

Meanwhile, Mr Chuckles turned to Rachel and Kirsty. "Is it OK if I set up my stuff in the lounge?" he asked.

Kirsty nodded. "Yes, we've almost finished decorating," she replied. "We've just got the balloons to blow up."

The clown opened the back of his van

and began to unload his props, while the girls went back into the lounge. But to their dismay, the streamers which they had so carefully pinned up earlier had all fallen down. Now they lay in heaps on the floor.

"This has to be the work of one of Jack Frost's goblins!" Rachel said crossly, grabbing a streamer. "He must be here somewhere."

"Quick, let's get these back up or Jamie will be upset," Kirsty said, picking up the sticky-tape.

The girls worked fast and got the streamers back in place before Jamie came bouncing into the room.

"We're going to blow up the balloons now, Jamie," said Kirsty, opening one of the packets. "Which colour shall we start with?"

"Gold!" Jamie called eagerly.

Kirsty began to blow air into the long gold balloon. But although she huffed and puffed and got red in the face, the balloon wouldn't inflate. It remained as flat as a pancake.

"There's a hole in it," Rachel said, peering closely at the balloon.

The girls exchanged a look. They were both thinking exactly the same thing.

"The goblin again!" Kirsty whispered. Quickly, she and Rachel checked all the other balloons. There were holes in all of them! Jamie's bottom lip was trembling. "Are all the balloons spoiled?" he asked in a small voice.

At that moment, Mr Chuckles came into the lounge carrying a large wooden box. "Is it balloons you need?" he asked. "I've got some spares." He put his hand into his pocket and pulled out a handful of different-coloured balloons. "I use them to make my balloon animals."

Kirsty and Rachel were very relieved to see Jamie smiling again. Quickly, they blew up the balloons and hung them around the French windows at the far end of the room.

Suddenly, the doorbell rang. Jamie peeped out of the front window. "It's Matthew, my best friend!" he shouted excitedly. "And Katie and Andy and Ben. It's time for my party to start!" And he dashed out to meet his guests.

"Goodness me, I must go to the bathroom and put my clown make-up on," said Mr Chuckles. He grabbed a small case and left the room.

POP! POP! POP!

Kirsty and Rachel jumped and turned round. The balloons they had just put up were bursting, one by one.

"I'm starting to get very fed up with that goblin," Rachel said crossly.

"So am I," Kirsty agreed. "We need to find him and put a stop to his tricks!"

The doorbell was ringing again as more guests arrived, and the girls could hear them chattering excitedly in the hall. They didn't have much time to find and stop the goblin.

Then they heard Mr Cooper's voice. "Follow me out to the garden, kids," he was saying. "We're going to have a treasure hunt!"

There was a loud cheer as the children hurried after him, and Rachel and Kirsty looked at each other in relief.

"Let's search the room," Kirsty suggested. "We might be able to deal with the goblin while everyone's in the garden."

But just as they began their search, Rachel groaned with dismay and clutched Kirsty's arm.

"What is it?" Kirsty whispered.

"Look!" Rachel said, pointing towards the French windows. "Outside in the garden."

Kirsty peered through the glass to see a sparkling pink shape flying swiftly through the air. It was zooming straight through the garden, towards the French windows of the lounge.

"Oh!" Kirsty gasped. "It's Grace the Glitter Fairy!"

"Yes," said Rachel anxiously. "And the children are going out into the garden. They'll all see her unless we do something – and fast!"

Saving Grace

"We have to go outside and warn her," Kirsty said.

"What about the goblin?" Rachel asked.

"This is more important," Kirsty replied, opening the French windows. She and Rachel rushed outside, waving their arms madly to get Grace's attention.

Grace saw them straightaway and
waved her sparkling pink wand at
them. She had long, straight, glossy
blonde hair, and she wore a glittering
rose-coloured dress, which shimmered in
the sunshine. The hem of the dress was
red and cut into handkerchief points.
The floaty skirt swirled around her legs
as she hovered in mid-air.

"Hello, girls," she called, "It's good to see you—"

"Grace, you have to hide!" Kirsty burst out, without even saying hello. "The party guests are about to come out into the garden any minute!"

Before Grace could say anything, they heard the back door open.

"So that's what you have to do, kids," Mr Cooper was saying. "Off you go."

Grace looked alarmed as all the children came galloping out of the back door. "Thanks for warning me, girls," she gasped. And she fluttered out of sight behind a garden urn filled with flowers.

The children were running all round
the garden now, screaming with
excitement. Two little girls came over
to where Kirsty and Rachel were
standing, and began to search for
presents there.

"Er, I think Mr Cooper hid most of
the presents down the bottom of the
garden," Rachel said quickly. She
didn't want the little girls poking
around and finding Grace.

One of the girls ran off straight away, but the other one frowned. "I can see something sparkly behind that pot," she said stubbornly, pointing at the urn. "It might be one of the presents."

"Oh, no," Kirsty said, thinking fast. She bent down and picked Grace up, keeping the fairy out of sight in her hand. Then she popped her in her pocket. "That's just an empty sweetie wrapper."

"We'll put it in the bin with the rubbish," Rachel added.

The girl looked disappointed and ran off after her friend. Kirsty and Rachel sighed with relief.

"Rubbish?" Grace said, poking her head out of Kirsty's pocket. She looked a bit flustered and her hair was all messy. "That's nice!"

"Sorry, Grace," Kirsty said soothingly. "We didn't mean it."

"There's a goblin here," Rachel told Grace, as the little fairy smoothed down her hair. "He's been ruining all the party decorations in the lounge."

"Well, we'll soon put a stop to that!" Grace declared, looking outraged.

"Where is he?"

"We don't know," Kirsty replied. "We were just about to start looking for him, when we saw you coming."

Grace nodded. "Well, now I can help you find him," she said, smiling. "Lead the way!"

As Kirsty led the way through the French windows into the lounge, she suddenly gasped and caught Rachel's arm. "Look, there!" she breathed. "Behind the curtain."

Rachel and Grace looked at the long blue curtains hanging either side of the French windows, and immediately saw what Kirsty had spotted – behind one of them, there was a definite goblin-shape!

An Uninvited Guest

They all stared at the goblin bulge
behind the curtain. They saw it
shift once or twice. The goblin
was obviously getting a bit fed up.

Kirsty beckoned Rachel and Grace
to follow her to the other end of the
room. "We need to do something
right now," Kirsty whispered.

"Before Jamie and his friends come in from the garden."

"Yes, but what?" Grace queried, biting her lip anxiously.
The three friends racked their brains to think of a plan.

"We could creep up on the goblin and grab him while he's wrapped in the curtain," Rachel suggested. "It shouldn't be too difficult. He's quite small." Rachel knew that Jack Frost's magic could make the goblins much bigger and scarier when they were in the human world, but as the Fairy King and Queen had taken Jack Frost's magic away for one year, the goblins were their normal size.

"Then Grace can quickly magic him
away to Fairyland," Rachel added.

Grace nodded enthusiastically, but
Kirsty looked worried. "He'll try to
fight his way out," she said. "What if
he ruins the curtain?"

"Well, it's made of really thick
material," Rachel pointed out. "I don't
think the goblin will be able to do
much damage."

"And I can fix it with
Fairy magic once I'm
back in Fairyland,"
put in Grace. "And
then I'll whiz back
here and magic it into
place for you, too."

"OK, let's give it a try,"
Kirsty agreed.

She and Rachel crept cautiously
towards the French windows, with
Grace fluttering alongside. They had
nearly reached the goblin, when the
lounge door suddenly opened and
Mrs Cooper appeared, laden with
plates of food.

Quick as a flash,
Grace darted
into Kirsty's
pocket, out
of sight.

"Ah, girls,"
said Jamie's mum.
"Could you possibly
give me a hand with these snacks?"

Rachel and Kirsty exchanged an
agonised look, but there was nothing
they could do.

"Yes, of course," Kirsty replied
politely, and the girls hurried to help
Mrs Cooper set the plates down on the
dining table.

"As soon as the children have finished
the treasure hunt, we'll bring them
in here," Mrs Cooper told the girls.

"They can have a snack before they watch Mr Chuckles, and then after his show, we'll have tea."

The girls nodded and Mrs Cooper headed back to the kitchen.

As soon as she had gone, Grace fluttered out of Kirsty's pocket and the girls turned back to tackle the goblin. But it was too late!

"Oh, no!" gasped Rachel, as she looked around the room. All the streamers lay on the floor again. The decorations were ruined. But, worse than that, the goblin-shape behind the curtain had vanished!

"Well, at least I can set these decorations to rights," Grace said, reaching into her pocket for her party bag.

But Kirsty stopped her. "No, you mustn't," she said in a low voice. "That's exactly what the goblin wants you to do. He's hiding somewhere – just waiting for the chance to snatch your party bag!"

Goblin Trap!

At that very moment, the three friends heard a scrabbling noise behind the sofa!

"The goblin must be hiding over there," Rachel whispered excitedly, pointing to the sofa. "And he's heard us talking about the party bag."

Kirsty's face lit up. "That's it!" she whispered. "We'll use Grace's party bag as bait to catch the goblin."

"I know how we can grab him, too,"
Rachel added quietly. She pointed
at the paper tablecloth,
which Mrs Cooper
had bought for
the party. "We'll
wrap him up
in the tablecloth
instead of the
curtain, and then Grace

can still whisk him off to Fairyland!"

"Good idea," Grace whispered.
"We'll hide behind that armchair, and
catch him red-handed." Then she spoke
again in a louder voice. "My party
bag's so heavy, girls," she said with a
wink. "It's because I've got so much
magic fairy dust in it."

"Why don't you put it down on the coffee table?" Rachel suggested, glancing at the sofa.

"Then you can come into the kitchen with us, and we'll show you Jamie's beautiful birthday cake," added Kirsty, picking up the shiny, gold-coloured tablecloth. "It's in the shape of a steam train."

"OK," Grace agreed. She pulled her sparkly blue party bag from her pocket, and placed it carefully on the coffee table. "Let's go then."

But instead of leaving the room, they all tiptoed over to the armchair, and hid behind it. It was a bit of a squash. Kirsty and Rachel were too big to both fit behind the chair.

"Rachel, your feet are sticking out," Grace whispered. "Wait a moment."

She twirled her blue wand in the air and there was a sparkle of fairy dust. In a second, Rachel and Kirsty had shrunk to fairy-size, with glittering wings on their backs. As tiny fairies, it was easy for all three friends to fit behind the armchair. Kirsty fluttered her wings happily.

Grace looked pleased. "That's better," she said, glancing at the sofa. "And we're just in time. Here he comes..."

The goblin poked his head round the edge of the sofa to see if the coast was clear. Then he stepped out, a big grin on his mean face. His beady little eyes gleamed as he saw the party bag lying on the coffee table, and he hurried to pick it up. "Jack Frost will be really pleased with me," the goblin chortled smugly.

But as he reached for the party bag, Grace, Kirsty and Rachel zoomed out of their hiding place, each holding a corner of the tablecloth.

"Get him!" Rachel yelled.

They hovered above the surprised
goblin, and dropped the tablecloth right
over him. He gave a shout of fury as it
covered him completely from head to toe.

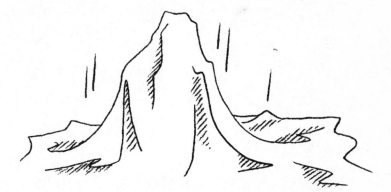

"It worked!" cried Kirsty.

"Now, let's wrap him up more
tightly," Grace said.

But before they do so, the goblin
began to rip the tablecloth to shreds!

All Wrapped Up!

"He's tearing his way out!" Kirsty
exclaimed. "What shall we do?"

Rachel looked round, spotted the streamers
on the floor and had an idea. She grabbed
the end of one of them, and flew swiftly
round and round the goblin, tying him up.

"Quick, Kirsty!" Grace called, as she saw
what Rachel was doing. "Grab a streamer."

"Stop it!" the goblin called crossly. He tried to fight his way out, but Grace and the girls were wrapping him up too quickly. A few minutes later he couldn't move. He looked just like an Egyptian mummy.

"Ohhh!" the goblin groaned sulkily.

"Serves you right," Rachel told him, as Grace rescued her precious party bag.

Meanwhile, Kirsty had fluttered over to the French windows to check on the treasure hunt.

"OK, kids, you've found all the presents," Mr Cooper was saying. "Now it's time to see Mr Chuckles, the clown."

"Jamie and his friends are coming in now, Grace," Kirsty called. "You'd better go."

Grace turned to the goblin. "And you're coming with me," she laughed. She waved her wand, and the moaning, grumbling goblin disappeared in a cloud of sparkling fairy dust.

"Goodbye, girls, and thank you," Grace said. She gave them a hug, and with a wave of her wand, made them human-sized again.

Then Kirsty remembered the decorations. "Grace, can you help?" she asked, pointing at the streamers and balloons.

Grace nodded and smiled. She tipped up her party bag, and emptied all the fairy dust into the lounge. Tiny, shining diamonds whirled and swirled around the room, spinning into every corner.

When the magic dust had cleared, Kirsty and Rachel were delighted to see that the walls were festooned with glittering, rainbow-coloured streamers and balloons.

There was even a new, gold, paper
tablecloth, and when Kirsty and Rachel
spread it out on the table, they saw
that it was shinier than before and
covered with a sprinkling of gleaming
silver stars.

"Thank you!" the girls cried in
amazement.

Grace gave a silvery laugh, waved her wand and disappeared, just as the children charged in led by Mr Cooper. They all stopped and stared in amazement at the fabulous decorations.

"Wow!" Jamie gasped. "Look what Kirsty and Rachel have done, Dad!"

"It's fantastic, girls," said Mr Cooper gratefully.

Rachel and Kirsty beamed at each
other, and sat down with the party
guests to watch Mr Chuckles perform.
The clown was very funny and had
everyone in fits of laughter with a
giant, water-squirting sunflower. Rachel
and Kirsty enjoyed it just as much as
Jamie and his friends.

At the end of the show, Mr Chuckles told them he was going to make some balloon animals. When he opened his bag and pulled out a handful of balloons, there was a gasp of wonder. They were the most wonderful, colourful balloons anyone had ever seen – and some were even striped and spotted with animal-print designs.

Mr Chuckles stared at them in
delight. "I didn't even know I had
these," he muttered.

Rachel and Kirsty smiled. They
knew where those balloons had come
from – Grace the Glitter Fairy!

Mr Chuckles began to twist and tie
the balloons together. He
made an elephant first,
which he gave to
Jamie. Then he
made a lovely
giraffe and a zebra.

"These are for the
two girls who put up
these beautiful decorations,"
Mr Chuckles said. He bowed, and
presented the giraffe to Rachel and the
zebra to Kirsty. The girls were thrilled.

And so was somebody else...

"This is my best birthday ever!" Jamie beamed, as the clown began to make animals for all the other children.

"And we've saved another Party Fairy and her party bag," Rachel whispered happily to Kirsty. "Hurray!"

The Party Fairies

Cherry, Melodie and Grace have got
their magic party bags back. Now
Rachel and Kirsty must help

Honey the Sweet Fairy

Win a Rainbow Magic
Sparkly T-Shirt and Goody Bag!

In every book in the Rainbow Magic Party Fairies series (books 15-21) there is a hidden picture of a magic party bag with a secret letter in it. Find all seven letters and re-arrange them to make a special Fairyland word, then send it to us. Each month we will put the entries into a draw and select one winner to receive a Rainbow Magic Sparkly T-shirt and Goody Bag!

Send your entry on a postcard to Rainbow Magic Competition, Orchard Books, 96 Leonard Street, London EC2A 4XD. Australian readers should write to Level 17/207 Kent St, Sydney, NSW 2000. Don't forget to include your name and address. Only one entry per child. Final draw: 28th April 2006.

Coming Soon...
The Jewel Fairies

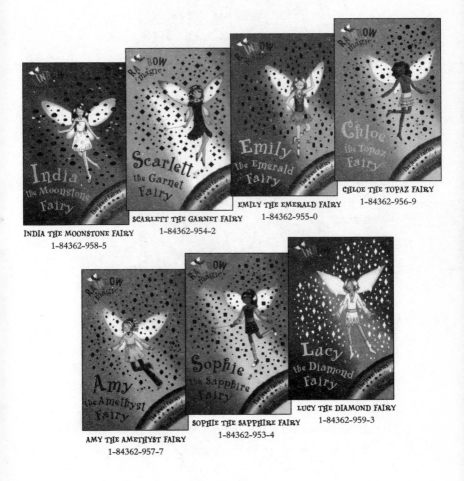

INDIA THE MOONSTONE FAIRY
1-84362-958-5

SCARLETT THE GARNET FAIRY
1-84362-954-2

EMILY THE EMERALD FAIRY
1-84362-955-0

CHLOE THE TOPAZ FAIRY
1-84362-956-9

AMY THE AMETHYST FAIRY
1-84362-957-7

SOPHIE THE SAPPHIRE FAIRY
1-84362-953-4

LUCY THE DIAMOND FAIRY
1-84362-959-3

Also coming soon . . .

SUMMER THE HOLIDAY FAIRY

1-84362-638-1

Summer the Holiday Fairy is getting all hot and bothered, trying to keep Rainspell Island the best place to go on vacation. Jack Frost has stolen the sand from the beaches, and three magical shells. The fairies need Rachel and Kirsty's help to get the holiday magic back...

Have you checked out the

Website at:
www.rainbowmagic.co.uk

There are games, activities and
fun things to do, as well as news
and information about Rainbow
Magic and all of the fairies.

RAINBOW magic

by Daisy Meadows

Ruby the Red Fairy	ISBN	1 84362 016 2
Amber the Orange Fairy	ISBN	1 84362 017 0
Saffron the Yellow Fairy	ISBN	1 84362 018 9
Fern the Green Fairy	ISBN	1 84362 019 7
Sky the Blue Fairy	ISBN	1 84362 020 0
Izzy the Indigo Fairy	ISBN	1 84362 021 9
Heather the Violet Fairy	ISBN	1 84362 022 7

The Weather Fairies

Crystal the Snow Fairy	ISBN	1 84362 633 0
Abigail the Breeze Fairy	ISBN	1 84362 634 9
Pearl the Cloud Fairy	ISBN	1 84362 635 7
Goldie the Sunshine Fairy	ISBN	1 84362 641 1
Evie the Mist Fairy	ISBN	1 84362 636 5
Storm the Lightning Fairy	ISBN	1 84362 637 3
Hayley the Rain Fairy	ISBN	1 84362 638 1

The Party Fairies

Cherry the Cake Fairy	ISBN	1 84362 818 X
Melodie the Music Fairy	ISBN	1 84362 819 8
Grace the Glitter Fairy	ISBN	1 84362 820 1
Honey the Sweet Fairy	ISBN	1 84362 821 X
Polly the Party Fun Fairy	ISBN	1 84362 822 8
Phoebe the Fashion Fairy	ISBN	1 84362 823 6
Jasmine the Present Fairy	ISBN	1 84362 824 4
Holly the Christmas Fairy	ISBN	1 84362 661 6

All priced at £3.99. Holly the Christmas Fairy priced at £4.99.
Rainbow Magic books are available from all good bookshops, or can be ordered
direct from the publisher: Orchard Books, PO BOX 29, Douglas IM99 1BQ
Credit card orders please telephone 01624 836000
or fax 01624 837033 or visit our Internet site: www.wattspub.co.uk
or e-mail: bookshop@enterprise.net for details.

To order please quote title, author and ISBN and your full name and address.
Cheques and postal orders should be made payable to 'Bookpost plc.'
Postage and packing is FREE within the UK
(overseas customers should add £2.00 per book).
Prices and availability are subject to change.